TOO
TALL
TINA

Ilff

Too-Tall Tina

Kane Press, Inc.
New York

Thank you, Michael, Brianna, and Christine.
Your encouragement makes me feel ten feet tall!—D.P.

Book Design/Art Direction: Roberta Pressel

Library of Congress Cataloging-in-Publication Data

Pitino, Donna Marie.
  Too-Tall Tina / by Donna Marie Pitino; illustrated by Liza Woodruff.
    p. cm. —(Math matters)
  "Comparing measurements—grades: K–2."
  Summary: Initially unhappy that a summer growth spurt has made her the tallest third grader at school, Tina soon realizes the advantages of being able to jump, reach, and step farther than her peers.
  ISBN 1-57565-150-5 (pbk. : alk. paper)
  [1. Measurement—Fiction. 2. Size—Fiction. 3. Growth—Fiction. 4. Self-acceptance—Fiction.]
I. Woodruff, Liza, ill. II. Title. III. Series.
  PZ7.P6456Too 2005
  [E]--dc22
                                2005004554

10 9 8 7 6 5 4 3 2 1

First published in the United States of America in 2005 by Kane Press, Inc.
Printed in Hong Kong.

MATH MATTERS is a registered trademark of Kane Press, Inc.

www.kanepress.com

Something happened to me this summer.
I *grew*. I grew taller and taller and taller!

I went to see Dr. Tasso for my checkup. "Wow, Tina!" she said. "That's some growth spurt you've had!"

I felt proud!

But on the first day of school, I stop feeling so great.

I used to be as tall as my two best
friends. Now I'm taller than Nancy. I'm
taller than Luke. I'm the tallest kid
in third grade!

tall   taller   tallest

I say hi to Mike.

"Hi, Tina!" he says. Then he looks up at me.
"Whoa, I mean—*Too-Tall Tina!*"

"How's the weather up there?" Anna asks.

Mike and Anna laugh.

I don't think they're very funny.

At recess I find my favorite jump rope from last year. It's purple with sparkly handles. I take a big jump, and— *Crash!* My favorite jump rope is too short for me.

Maybe Mike is right. Maybe I *am* Too-Tall Tina.

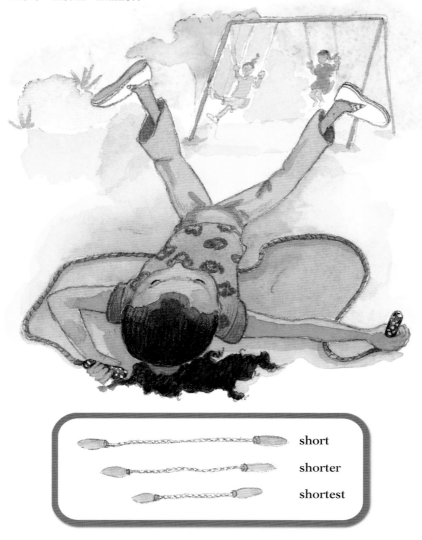

short

shorter

shortest

Nancy and Luke help me up.

"Thanks," I mumble.

"Don't worry," Luke says. "You just need a longer rope!"

I try to smile.

It's almost time to go home.

"Don't forget, Friday is Class Picture Day," Mr. Lee reminds us. "Let's make Grade 3 look sharp."

All the kids are excited—except me.

The lady who takes our picture always lines us up by how tall we are. Nancy and Luke and I are next to each other every year. But not *this* year.

"I don't want to be in the back row, away from you guys," I moan.

"Maybe you'll like the back row," says Nancy.

"Yeah! When you're in the back, no one can tell if your socks are dirty!" Luke adds.

"But we're *always* together—like the Three Musketeers," I reply.

Nancy and Luke shrug sadly.

That night I get to thinking.

Aha! I know what to do. I go to my closet, and . . . *Yes!* These are perfect! Nancy and Luke will be as tall as I am on Picture Day.

Before school starts, I tell Luke and Nancy my idea.

"*Girls'* shoes?"
Luke gasps. "No way!"

"Oooh! High heels," says Nancy. She puts them on and starts to walk.

Wobble, wobble— *Plop!* She falls, and lands with a thud.
So much for Plan A.

It's time for Plan B.

I tuck my head in. I bend my knees. I squish myself down and waddle over to Luke.

"Now I'm as short as you are!" I tell him.

"Yeah," Luke says. "But you look like a duck."

That's not good. I stand back up.

"Hey, guys!" calls Felix. "Want to play limbo?"

"All right!" Nancy and Luke yell. They rush over. I follow—slowly.

Last year I was super at limbo. I'd scoot right under the stick—even when it was really, really low.

But now I'm Too-Tall Tina.

When my turn comes, I take a deep breath. I bend my knees lower and lower. I lean back farther and farther. I'm halfway under the stick! I lean back just a little more—

low   lower   lowest

Splat!
I feel like crying.
I get up and walk away.
Nancy and Luke follow me.

"There's *nothing* good about being tall,"
I complain.

"That's not true," Luke says. "You can see
over everybody's head at parades!"

"And reach the cookies on the top shelf!"
adds Nancy.

"I guess so," I say. But I still feel bad.

"I know what will cheer you up," Luke says. "Tomorrow is Sports Day. You love Sports Day!"

I *do* love Sports Day. Well, I *used* to love it—just like I used to love jumping rope and playing limbo.

But now I'm Too-Tall Tina.

Sports Day starts first thing in the morning. Our gym teacher, Ms. Como, puts me on the Orange Team with Nancy and Luke. *Hmm.* Maybe this won't be so bad after all.

"The pole climb is first," Ms. Como says. "Whoever climbs the highest gets a point for his or her team!"

Uh-oh! I'm not so great at pole climbing.

It's my turn. I gulp hard, grab the pole,
and pull myself up. I pull and pull.

"Time's up!" Ms. Como calls out.

I look down. I didn't get very far. Oh, well.
At least I didn't fall off the pole!

"That's one point for the Green Team,"
says Ms. Como.

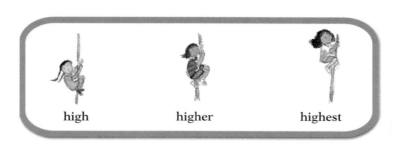

high   higher   highest

The next game is Giant Steps. It's me against Anna and Mike. We warm up.

"Whoever reaches the red line in the fewest number of steps wins a point," Ms. Como explains. "Ready, set— *Go!*"

I stretch my legs as far as I can and take a long step. Then I take another and another—all the way to the finish line.

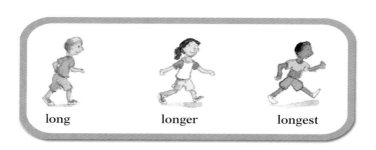

long   longer   longest

"Anna took ten steps, Mike took nine, and Tina took eight," Ms. Como says. "That means . . ."

I hold my breath.

"The Orange Team gets a point!"

My whole team starts to cheer. Nancy and Luke cheer the loudest.

Our last game is the long jump. The score is tied. "The team that makes the longest long-jump wins," says Ms. Como.

Luke goes first. He jumps far!

Then it's Mike's turn. He jumps farther.

The Green Team is in the lead. And I'm the last one to go.

I take a deep breath. I start to run. I close my eyes.

I jump!

My feet hit the ground. Where did I land? I'm too nervous to look.

"Way to go, Tina!" my team shouts.

I peek out of one eye. I did it! I jumped the farthest of anyone!

| far | farther | farthest |

"The Orange Team wins!" Ms. Como announces.

I'm so surprised I just keep standing in the sand pit with a smile on my face.

Ms. Como gives me a big blue ribbon!

More good things happen. On Thursday I find a *long* jump rope with red sparkly handles. It's perfect!

Then Mike's soccer ball gets stuck in a tree. Lots of kids try to reach it. But only *my* arms are long enough.

"Thanks, Too-Tall Tina! Er, I mean *Terrifically* Tall Tina!" Mike says.

"Tina, I'm going to make you our official
Class Reacher!" Mr. Lee says.

Nancy and Luke give me a thumbs up.

Finally it's Friday—Class Picture Day! And guess what? I don't mind being in the back row.

GOOD THINGS ABOUT BEING TALL

- You can take GIANT giant steps.
- Your long jumps are VERY long.
- You can see over everybody's head.
- You can reach stuff nobody else can.
- You get to sit in the back of class.
- You stand out in the class picture!

After all, I'm Terrifically Tall Tina!

COMPARING MEASUREMENTS CHART

You can use words to compare the three things in each row.

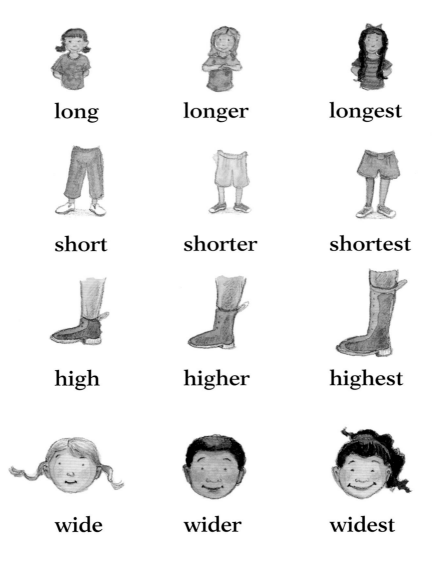

long	longer	longest
short	shorter	shortest
high	higher	highest
wide	wider	widest